For Cathleen With for teaching and inspiring creativity

Charming

METTE BACH

JAMES LORIMER & COMPANY LTD., PUBLISHERS
TORONTO

Published in Canada in 2018. Published in the United States in 2019.

James Lorimer & Company Ltd., Publishers acknowledges funding support from the Ontario Arts Council (OAC), an agency of the Government of Ontario. We acknowledge the support of the Canada Council for the Arts, which last year invested $153 million to bring the arts to Canadians throughout the country. This project has been made possible in part by the Government of Canada and with the support of the Ontario Media Development Corporation.

Canada

Cover design: Tyler Cleroux
Cover image: Shutterstock

Library and Archives Canada Cataloguing in Publication

Bach, Mette, 1976-, author
Charming / Mette Bach.

(Real love)
Issued in print and electronic formats.
ISBN 978-1-4594-1387-0 (softcover).--ISBN 978-1-4594-1388-7 (EPUB)

I. Title. II. Series: Real love (Series)

PS8603.A298C43 2018 jC813'.6 C2018-902561-1
C2018-902562-X

Published by:
James Lorimer & Company Ltd., Publishers
117 Peter Street, Suite 304
Toronto, ON, Canada
M5V 0M3
www.lorimer.ca

Distributed in Canada by:
Formac Lorimer Books
5502 Atlantic Street
Halifax, NS, Canada
B3H 1G4

Distributed in the US by:
Lerner Publisher Services
1251 Washington Ave. N.
Minneapolis, MN, USA
55401
www.lernerbooks.com

Printed and bound in Canada.
Manufactured by Friesens Corporation in Altona, Manitoba, Canada in July 2018.
Job # 245778

PROLOGUE

Viral

CHAR GILL WAS RIDING WITH HER MOM in the SUV. They had just loaded the car with stuff from Bed Bath & Beyond. Now her mom was chatting away about how she had to stage her next open house. She was explaining to Char how she used to hire stagers, but that it was easier to do it herself. Char's mom did everything herself, from manicures to taxes.

Char was staring at her phone.

"Put that away and help me navigate," her mom pleaded.

"That's what GPS is for," Char said.

"Do you even know how to read a map?" her mom snapped.

Char rolled her eyes. "Mom, this is important."

"So is making the right turnoff on the highway." They were on their way to the new outlet mall near the airport in Richmond. Char had tagged along because she wanted to check out shoes. But what was happening was way better than shoes.

"No, this is like, really, really important," Char insisted. She couldn't look away from her phone's screen. If she looked away, maybe it would all vanish.

"What is it?"

"Never mind."

There was no point in telling her mom. She wouldn't get it. There was just no way. But as they drove toward Richmond, Char saw her video get more than a hundred thumbs-up on YouTube in just twenty minutes. Everyone liked her cover of Rihanna's "FourFiveSeconds." At this rate Char would be famous before graduation.

That was the goal. That would set her up for a future. It wasn't just Char's goal, it was everyone's goal. But Char was the one on the path. And that was something she couldn't look away from for even a second.

01 All the Likes

CHAR TILTED HER PHONE EVER SO SLIGHTLY to the left. It was maybe her tenth try for a perfect selfie with her morning skim milk latte. She tapped on the cup with one of the fake nails she applied to hide her own bitten ones. It was hard to keep coming up with new stuff to post. The other girls at school seemed to find it easy. When you looked at their lives, everything seemed glamorous and beautiful. It wasn't that Char's latte wasn't good, but how could she get across how to queer youth events downtown or take part in the LGBTQ+ club at school. But it got too hard for her to defend herself for not being out. So now she spent all her free time thinking up ways to get back the excitement of instant fame. She'd never felt anything like it. Char, who had never done anything special, was a sensation. She had gone viral.

The problem with knowing that kind of bliss was getting it to happen again. Char never would have thought about it in the first place. But now she was showing the world her purchases at Lush, talking about the smell of bath bombs while she demoed scrubs on her hand. She had made a few videos of makeup tutorials and her evening skin care routine. But nothing passed one thousand views. What could she do to get those numbers back?

By the time two o'clock rolled around, Char was so tired from not paying attention in her classes that she

"That'll never happen. They'll be mad for a while. But I'll win them over. I am Charming, after all."

Ash snorted when she laughed. "Yeah, you are."

"Can we do this, Ash?" Char asked, suddenly serious. "Your scholarship money would go much farther just for you. Do you really want my future dragging down yours?"

Ash's laugh had turned into a gentle smile. "I could be asking you the same thing, Char. You're doing the same work I was doing in the cafeteria. You're giving up your Fiat and your home. Will you give up online fame and being popular for hard work and little recognition? Will you give up your family, even for a while, for me?"

Char knew the answer before Ash had even finished. "Happily," said. And she sealed the word with a kiss.

Acknowledgements

To Kat Mototsune, editor extraordinaire, I am grateful for the many delightful and insightful conversations. Working with you is the best. To everyone else at Lorimer, thank you for all of the support with this project.

To Tony Correia, Andrea Warner, Billeh Nickerson, Jackie Wong, Cathleen With, Monica Meneghetti, Karen X Tulchinsky, Angela Short, and Shana Myara, you kept me going, and talked me through plot problems and life problems. There is no adequate thank you for your wisdom and support.

My besties from the olden days, Cecilia Leong and Elaine Yong, you kept me sane (relatively) in the midst of chaos. I'm grateful for my wonderful co-workers at Directions Youth Services Centre and the resilient youth who chat with me there; you provide endless inspiration every day.

To my mom, with her broken hip and speedy recovery, thank you for showing me mental strength and determination. To Maria Callahan, who put me in a cowboy hat and drove me across America, thank you for showing me what it means to have a musician's heart.